COMIC CHAPTER BOOKS

SUPERMAN

STONE ARCH BOOKS
a capstone imprint

Superman: Comic Chapter Books are published by
Stone Arch Books,
A Capstone Imprint
1710 Roe Crest Drive
North Mankato, Minnesota 56003
www.capstoneyoungreaders.com

Star33640

Library of Congress Cataloging-in-Publication Data is
available on the Library of Congress website.

ISBN: 978-1-4965-0509-5 (library binding)
ISBN: 978-1-4965-0511-8 (paperback
ISBN: 978-1-4965-2302-0 (eBook)

Summary: There are few places more dangerous than
Apokolips, but Superman never turns away from those
who need help. The downtrodden slaves of the planet,
known as the Lowlies, are ready to throw off their
shackles, but first Superman and the freedom fighters
must battle Darkseid's forces to ensure the slaves'
freedom. They'll face Parademons, Female Furries, and
the most fearsome villain in the universe — Darkseid
himself. Is Superman strong enough to defeat the evil
super-villain, or are some challenges too great for even
the Man of Steel?

Printed in Canada.
052015   008825FRF15

COMIC CHAPTER BOOKS

DC COMICS SUPER HEROES

SUPERMAN

THE DARK SIDE OF APOKOLIPS

written by
Laurie S. Sutton

illustrated by
Luciano Vecchio

Superman created by Jerry Siegel and Joe Shuster
By special arrangement with the Jerry Siegel family

TABLE OF CONTENTS

CHAPTER 1
A CALL FOR HELP 7

CHAPTER 2
APOKOLIPS 21

CHAPTER 3
REBEL BASE 35

CHAPTER 4
FIGHT FOR FREEDOM 51

CHAPTER 5
ALL OR NOTHING 65

 A CALL FOR HELP

"Emergency! Emergency!" the pilot called out over the radio.

The police helicopter was spinning around and around, out of control.

"I've been hit! I'm going down," the pilot shouted. "Mayday, mayday!"

All the instruments on the control panel either blinked red or were dark and useless. Thick black smoke poured out of the engine. A large, charred streak was on the side of the helicopter where it had been hit. The pilot still wasn't sure what had struck him.

Suddenly, the helicopter stopped falling! The pilot tensed in his seat as the aircraft halted in midair. "How is this possible?" he asked no one in particular.

Superman was holding one of the helicopter's landing struts. "Don't worry," he said. "I've got you."

The pilot cheered. "Superman!" he cried. "Thank you!"

The Man of Steel descended through the air with the helicopter in one hand. He set it down safely in an empty baseball field. Then he helped the pilot climb out of the cockpit.

Superman examined the blast marks on the side of the helicopter. "What happened?" he asked.

"I was responding to a report of flying monsters or aliens," the police pilot said. "I don't know which because I never got to the scene. Before I got there, something hit my chopper."

"Monsters? Aliens?" Superman said. He scanned the surrounding skies with his telescopic vision. He frowned at what he saw. "Hmm. I'd say it's a little bit of both."

The Man of Steel leaped into the air.

"Superman, wait!" the pilot shouted.

The Man of Steel paused and hovered in midair. "What is it?" he asked.

"How can I help?" the police pilot asked.

"Stay here and keep people calm and safe," replied the Earth's Mightiest Hero. "This is a job for Superman!"

The Man of Steel sped toward trouble. The pilot had been right, in a way: the perpetrators were both aliens and monsters in one combined form.

"Parademons!" Superman said as he arrived at a scene of aerial battle.

"We're surrounded!" the strange woman said.

A moment later, the Parademons had grabbed hold of both Superman and the flying warrior.

FLEX!

Superman tensed his super-strong muscles and burst out of the cocoon of Darkseid's alien warriors. They came back for more immediately.

SMACK!

POW!

The Man of Steel punched his opponents one by one. They were knocked away, but they kept returning.

Suddenly, a powerful energy blast hit the Parademons.

KA-BLAAAAM!

The woman warrior fired her club at her foes. They fell out of the sky and landed in a lake below.

Superman wondered if it was the woman's power club that had blasted the helicopter. Was she a friend or foe?

"Who are you?" Superman asked again.

"My name is Atheena. I need your help," the woman said.

That was all she had a chance to say. A Parademon streaked up from below and blasted Atheena with a power rod.

KRACKLE!

Unconscious, Atheena dropped out of the sky and into the Parademon's arms. Superman was surprised to see that the alien warrior didn't try to hurt Atheena, since Darkseid's soldiers were not known to show mercy. The Parademon flew away with his captive, completely ignoring Superman.

The Man of Steel took off in pursuit. He

was about to slam into the alien abductor when the rest of the troop surged up from below. Superman was surrounded.

The Man of Steel wasn't about to stop his chase. Instead, he started to twirl like a corkscrew through the sky. His motion churned up the air and created a sideways tornado.

WOOSH! SWOOSH!

The Parademons were tossed away.

At last Superman saw where the Parademon was taking Atheena: a Boom Tube looming in the distance. The glowing energy tunnel floated high in the sky.

"That's strange," Superman said. "A Boom Tube doesn't usually stay open once people come through it."

He couldn't worry about that now. The Parademon was going to take Atheena through the teleportation portal. It almost certainly led to the planet Apokolips.

The alien soldier didn't expect an attack from his unconscious captive. He was stunned and fell back to Earth like the rest of his troop.

Atheena nodded at the Man of Steel. "Thank you, Superman," she said. Atheena glanced at the glowing Boom Tube. "The portal won't last very long. I have to get back to Apokolips."

"Wait — you *want* to go to Apokolips?" Superman asked, confused. "I thought I was saving you from that fate. You said you wanted my help."

"I do need your help — come with me to Darkseid's realm!" Atheena said. "I need your assistance against the forces of Darkseid!"

As the Boom Tube hummed with power behind them, Atheena quickly explained her predicament. "I am a freedom fighter on Apokolips," she said.

"As far as I know, the concept of *freedom* doesn't even exist on Darkseid's world, let alone a freedom fighter," Superman said.

"I know. I am the first," Atheena said proudly.

"How? Darkseid rules with such cruelty," the Man of Steel said in a grim voice. "I've been to Apokolips."

"Yes, and that is what inspired me!" Atheena said. "See, I saw you there. I was one of the Lowlies. I worked as a drone beneath the cold glare of the Dark Lord. But I saw you fight him! You inspired me, Superman. You fought Darkseid. So I decided to fight him, too."

Atheena clasped the Man of Steel by the arms. "I don't have superpowers like you, but I have a small army of rebels," she told him. "We have a plan, but we need your help to put it into motion."

"Tell me about this plan," Superman said.

Atheena explained her plot to the Man of Steel between urgent glances at the shrinking Boom Tube behind them.

When she had finished, Superman rubbed his chin. "It sounds dangerous — but also very courageous," he said after a moment. "I'll help you."

"Wonderful!" Atheena said. "We should leave at once. The Boom Tube won't stay open much longer."

"There's one thing I have to do first," Superman said.

SWOOOOOOOSH!

The Man of Steel sped away in a blur, leaving Atheena hovering in front of the energy portal. When he returned, he had the defeated Parademons all wrapped up in a net made of steel cables.

"I had to clean up the mess we made," Superman said. "And I couldn't leave Parademons scattered around the landscape. They'd just get into more trouble while I was gone."

"Good thing you're fast!" Atheena said.

Together, they entered the Boom Tube. It closed behind them with a big **BOOM!**

CHAPTER 2

APOKOLIPS

Atheena and Superman stood at the other end of the Boom Tube and looked out over Apokolips. The massive city was bleak, depressing, and dark. It was permanent nighttime on the planet. The only light came from the blazing Fire Pits below.

Superman stood inside the mouth of the energy portal. "This place hasn't changed," he said.

Atheena nodded. "With your help, it might," she said.

Atheena stepped out of the Boom Tube and onto the charred soil of Apokolips.

Superman moved away from the portal and hovered several feet off the ground. He held the net full of defeated Parademons in one fist. Once Atheena and the Man of Steel exited the Boom Tube, it closed with a loud BOOM!

The people on the streets paid no attention to the noise or to the new arrivals. They shuffled around Superman and Atheena, their minds too numb to react.

"They don't really have minds of their own anymore," Atheena explained. "Darkseid has taken away their wills, their hearts, and their hope."

Watching the poor souls shuffling along like zombies made Superman even more determined to help Atheena fight for their freedom.

"If a single Lowlie like you can rise up out of this darkness, then so can others," the Man of Steel declared. "I'll do everything in my power to help you."

Suddenly, a scream split the air. Superman reacted without a second thought. He dropped the net full of Parademons and flew to the rescue.

He arrived at the source of the shriek. It had come from an Apokolips nobleman with a very high voice.

"You Lowlie scum!" the man yelled at the slave who had collapsed at his feet. "You got mud on my robes!"

The Lowlie sprawled next to the heavy burden he had been carrying. Other Lowlies simply walked around the fallen drone and the bag he had dropped. No one made a move to help him.

"Lazy slave," the nobleman said. He raised his foot to kick the Lowlie — but stopped when he saw an imposing figure dressed in red and blue hovering in the air between him and the Lowlie.

WHEN SUPERMAN'S FOOT TOUCHES THE SURFACE OF APOKOLIPS...

I SENSE THE KRYPTONIAN IS HERE!

Darkseid's eyes burned with intense fury and hate. Superman had long been his archenemy. Darkseid considered him to be a menace to Apokolips. And the Dark Lord knew exactly how to take care of such threats . . .

"Parademons! Attack!" Darkseid commanded.

SWOOOSH! WOOOOSH!

The warriors standing guard next to Darkseid flew to do their master's bidding. At the same time, the Parademons trapped in the steel net heard their master's command and started to break loose from the steel cables.

SNAP SNAP SNAP
SNAP SNAP SNAP!

Atheena jumped back in surprise as the creatures tore through the net. "So, you still have some fight left in you?" she said, clenching her fists. "Then bring it!"

ZAP!

Atheena fired her energy club at the nearest soldier. The creature took the blast on his armor and kept on coming. A single blast from the soldier's energy rod hit Atheena's armor and knocked her backward.

SMASH!

She crashed into a crowd of mindless Lowlies. They barely reacted to the battle happening around them. Atheena slammed against a wall and her energy club fell from her numb fingers.

"You monsters just don't give up," Atheena grumbled as the Parademons marched toward her. "Neither do I."

Atheena struggled to grip her energy club. She could barely feel it in her hands, but that didn't stop her from firing it!

BLAM! A blast knocked all the Parademons off their feet. They struggled to stand up immediately. So did Atheena.

"Where's a super hero when you need one?" Atheena wondered as she wobbled on her feet.

Suddenly Superman zoomed out of the dark sky and smashed into the Parademons surrounding Atheena.

WHAM-BLAM!

"I heard the sound of weapons and thought there might be trouble," the Man of Steel said. "I see I'm right."

"Here comes more trouble," Atheena said. She pointed to a squadron of Parademons flying toward them.

Darkseid's Parademon guards zoomed down at Superman and Atheena, obeying their master's command to attack.

They did not know who their enemy was, nor did they care. They unleashed their energy weapons at their target in a mindless frenzy. The streets turned as bright as a small sun.

Superman used his body to block the onslaught of the powerful weapons.

ZZZZRT!

ZAP!

ZZZZRT!

Sizzling energy bounced off the Man of Steel. Atheena crouched behind him and covered her head, but soon covered her ears instead. The sound was deafening!

Parademons stood on opposite sides of Superman and Atheena. The soldiers aimed their energy rods and blasters at their enemies.

"Hold on to me!" Superman told Atheena. He grabbed her and leaped into the sky at super-speed.

The Parademons fired their weapons, but Superman and Atheena were no longer there. The energy blasts hit the Parademons on the other side instead!

The majority of the Parademons were down and out. But some soldiers managed to escape the blast. Now they flew after the Man of Steel and Atheena.

Atheena pointed below. "Take us down there!" she shouted to Superman. "I have a plan!"

The Man of Steel landed next to the searing flames of a massive Fire Pit.

SHOOM!
SHOOM!
SHOOM!

Huge tendrils of fire sprayed up and out from the pit.

The Parademons landed nearby. They pointed their weapons at Superman and Atheena. Superman and Atheena braced themselves for another battle.

Suddenly, the soldiers paused. It was as if they were listening to a silent voice.

"It's Darkseid!" Atheena realized. "He's delivering new orders to the Parademons."

"How do you know?" Superman asked.

"Because I can hear him, too," Atheena said. "He wants me alive."

"Then I need to get you out of here," the Man of Steel said.

"I have an exit planned," Atheena said. "I just hope it works! Quickly, follow me, Superman!"

Atheena started to crawl up the outside of the Fire Pit. The Parademons surged forward.

ZIP!
ZAP!

Atheena fired her energy club at the advancing troops. Superman launched himself at them, ready to deliver a super-strong punch.

KA-POW!
SCHING!

Energy blasts bounced off him like fireworks.

KA-POWWW!

The Man of Steel landed a blow on the Parademon attackers, scattering them like bowling pins.

Atheena shouted and pointed. "The other ones have recovered," she said. "Here they come!"

Atheena stepped up to the edge of the Fire Pit. "Get ready to follow me, Superman!" she said.

The Man of Steel didn't know what Atheena meant. Then he saw her fall into the Fire Pit!

"No!" shouted the Man of Steel. He leaped after Atheena, following her into the flames of Apokolips.

Darkseid would reprimand his Parademons for failing him later. But for now, he was confident in the knowledge that the Man of Steel was no more.

The Dark Lord smiled, a rare sight for the tyrant of Apokolips.

CHAPTER 3

REBEL BASE

"It worked!" Atheena said. She and Superman stood on a narrow ledge on the inside of the Fire Pit.

"You sound surprised," Superman said.

"I am, a little," Atheena admitted. "I wasn't sure which pit this was and where the hatch was located."

"Hatch?" Superman asked.

Atheena grinned. "I used to work in the Fire Pits. They're all built to the same design. There should be a maintenance hatch around here somewhere."

"You'd better find it fast," Superman said. "I'm invulnerable to the heat, but *you* aren't."

"I'm tougher than I look, but you're right," Atheena said.

She led Superman along the ledge. They crept slowly, inch by inch, as the Fire Pit's flames flared out at them.

FWOOSH!

Superman blew a puff of super-breath to deflect the molten tendrils of fire away from Atheena.

"Here we are!" Atheena said. She pulled on a small lever. An opening appeared in the wall of the Fire Pit.

An explosion of fire bloomed up from the pit. Even Superman could feel the heat rising. "Get inside!" he warned.

The Man of Steel shoved Atheena into the open hatch and protected her with his body.

The flare raced up the wall of the Fire Pit just as Superman slammed the hatch shut.

"That wasn't a scheduled flare," Atheena said. "But they sometimes happen."

"That would've been nice to know beforehand," Superman said with a smirk.

Atheena laughed. "Sorry!"

Superman and Atheena walked down a dim corridor. Soon they reached a junction where more corridors split off in different directions. Atheena did not choose any of them. She lifted a hatch in the floor and revealed a ladder leading down.

There was enough room for two people, so Superman floated next to Atheena as she descended. When they reached the bottom, they walked through another hatch.

Superman gazed at the incredible vista before them. "Where are we?" he asked.

"This is where I live . . ." Atheena began.

"... the Old Gods come one step closer to resurrection," Atheena finished. "If the Old Gods ever emerge, Darkseid will have his cold heart handed to him on a platter. It may never happen in my lifetime, but even the thought of goodness returning to this planet gives me hope."

Superman and Atheena came to a landing on the staircase. Atheena stopped and studied the surface of the cavern wall. After a moment she stretched out her hand and pressed it against a square-shaped groove in the rock.

BLEEP!

A panel lit up.

Superman tried to use his X-ray vision to see what was on the other side of the rock. "Why can't I see inside with my X-ray vision?" the Man of Steel asked.

"The Old Gods' technology blocks such things," Atheena said. "Their devices are still scattered around the Necropolis."

FWIRRRSSSSH!

A door opened in the wall to reveal an elevator. Superman raised an eyebrow.

Atheena smiled. "A shortcut," she said. "Did you think we were going to walk all the way down?"

"Well, I was going to fly down," Superman said. "But this will do nicely."

They stepped into the elevator pod. As soon as the door shut, the pod began to descend. Then it moved sideways. The elevator changed directions several times as if traveling through a maze.

Eventually the door opened to reveal another large cave. This one was not dark and gloomy. It was bright and filled with people.

"Atheena! Atheena is back!" someone shouted.

"HURRAH! HURRAH!"

Cheers filled the cavern. People rushed to surround Atheena and Superman.

"This is amazing," Superman said. "I've never seen so many happy faces on Apokolips. You really have created hope."

A single man pushed his way through the crowd to reach Superman and Atheena. As soon as Atheena saw him, she held out her arms and gave him a big hug. Superman thought he saw tears in Atheena's eyes.

"Atheena! You made it back — and with Superman!" the man said.

"I told you I would. Did you have any doubt?" Atheena asked.

The man shrugged, then laughed. Atheena stood and introduced the man to Superman. "Superman, this is Dr. Zox," she said. "He is crucial to our plan."

"I'm not important, but the robots are!" Zox insisted. "Let me show you."

The Man of Steel moved so fast that Atheena and Dr. Zox could barely follow him. Members of Atheena's freedom force gathered and watched in amazement as Superman worked.

"It took us weeks to assemble the prototype, but Superman is doing each one in a minute flat!" one woman said.

When he was finished, Superman landed next to Atheena and Dr. Zox. They nodded in approval.

"Does it meet your specs?" asked the Man of Steel.

"There's only one way to find out," Atheena said. She walked over to the new robot and climbed into the control pod.

ZWAP!

An energy blast fired from one of the cannons.

"Oops! Sorry!" Atheena shouted in apology. "The controls are more sensitive on this one. Superman made some improvements!"

"I tweaked the design a little," Superman said to Zox. "And installed some minor upgrades. I hope you don't mind."

"Not if it helps us to escape Darkseid's tyranny!" Zox said happily.

"Let's put this model to a full test. Battle Group One — attack!" Atheena shouted. "And don't hold back!"

A group of freedom fighters assembled in a flurry.

ZRRT!
ZAP!
BZZT!

They fired their energy weapons at the battle robot. The blasts simply bounced off the machine's surface.

Dr. Zox's eyes went wide. "No damage? But how?"

"A force field," Superman told Dr. Zox. "One of the little tweaks I made. It should protect the robot from most any kind of energy attack."

Atheena smiled in the control pod. She fired up the boot rockets.

WIRRRRRSH!

The robot ascended as far as it could in the cavern. Battle Group One continued to fire on the machine, but Atheena was not concerned. She fired the energy cannons at a target set up in the underground test site.

ZZZZRRRRRP!

The target disintegrated. The only thing left was a crater in the ground.

WHAM!

Atheena was rocked by an unexpected force.

Alarms sounded in the control pod. Atheena ignored them and looked around for what had hit her. She saw Superman floating in the air in front of the robot. He waved.

Atheena grinned in reply. "Challenge accepted," she said.

Atheena fired at Superman with a continuous blast from the energy cannons.

ZIP! ZAP! ZRRRRT! FWIRSH!

She launched missiles at the same time. The Man of Steel disappeared in a ball of flame and smoke. When it cleared, he still floated there with a smile on his face.

"I make a pretty good target," he said.

"This robot works perfectly," Atheena declared.

"Three hundred more, coming right up," Superman promised.

CHAPTER 4

FIGHT FOR FREEDOM

It had taken only a few hours for the Man of Steel to create the new robots at super-speed. Now, Superman and Atheena stood in front of an entire fleet of battle robots.

Freedom fighters climbed into the mechanisms and got comfortable with the controls. Cannons swiveled on their turrets and boot boosters roared.

"Thank you, Superman," Atheena said. "Without you, it would have taken us years to build this many robots. We've managed to stay hidden from Darkseid under the Fire Pits, but I don't know how long that will last."

"Can you hear him down here, like you can on the surface?" Superman asked.

"No. There's something about the Fire Pits that blocks the connection," Atheena said. "That has kept us safe so far, but Darkseid knows about me now. He will do everything in his power to find me."

"Then the Master Plan should begin immediately," Superman said. "Tell me what I can do."

"But you've already done so much! You've built a fleet of battle robots!" Atheena said. "We'll use them to battle the Parademons and give the freedom forces a chance to escape Apokolips."

"You haven't told me how you plan to leave the planet," Superman said. "You don't have a spaceship. The only other transport is by way of a Boom Tube, and you don't have a Mother Box to create one."

"We have something better!" Dr. Zox said.

He walked up to Superman and Atheena. A large cube was in his hands. "It's the Old Gods' technology," Dr. Zox said. "I found it while exploring in the Necropolis."

"What is it?" Superman asked. He tried to use his X-ray vision, but he couldn't see into the cube. "Just like the hidden elevator."

"It's an 'ancestor' of a Mother Box," Zox revealed with a nod.

BONG!

The cube responded with a deep tone.

Zox smiled. "I think it likes you, Superman!" he said. "The Grandmother Box opens a Boom Tube to other planets. That's how Atheena got to Earth to find you."

"The Grandmother Box can also open a portal to a sanctuary world," Atheena continued. "Once we're off Apokolips soil, Darkseid can't track us. We'll be safe."

Superman nodded in approval. It was a good plan. "Then let's get started," he said.

Superman was the first one out of the gate. He flew through the blazing hole and straight into the flames of a Fire Pit!

"Uh-oh!" Superman said. "That wasn't on the map."

"Sorry, Superman!" Atheena said to Superman through an earpiece. "That's another unscheduled flare. Darkseid must be angry!"

"When isn't he?" Superman said. "I have an idea . . ."

The Man of Steel plunged into the blaze and disappeared. Atheena gasped. Would he be destroyed? Without the Man of Steel, their plan wouldn't work.

Suddenly the flames of the Fire Pit were extinguished.

"Impossible!" Atheena said. "The flames are out! We must seize this opportunity. All freedom forces: move! The flames are out! Climb!"

The freedom fighters scrambled up the inside surface of the Fire Pit and crawled safely over its edge.

The robot fleet flew out of the gate and into clear air. Atheena hovered above the Fire Pit in her battle robot.

"Only Superman could have snuffed those flames. But did he sacrifice himself doing it? For us?" Atheena said anxiously.

"I'm just getting started," Superman's voice said in her earpiece.

Suddenly a blue and red blur streaked up out of the Fire Pit just ahead of a massive eruption.

BWAM!

Claws of flame reached for the sky. Fire filled the air in a volcanic explosion of hungry flames.

The Lowlies on the streets around the Fire Pit were struck by the wave of heat and fire. Some collapsed, overwhelmed by the blast. Others moaned but continued to shuffle along. They didn't know any other way of life than servitude.

But then one Lowlie looked up. She saw Superman flying overhead. She did not know what the strange creature was. She didn't know why she had looked up, but now that she had, she knew there was something more to life. Something better than living in fear and darkness.

But what the Lowlie sees, Darkseid does, too!

AT THE SAME TIME...

Darkseid raged at the holographic sight of Superman on his display. "The Kryptonian still lives!" he growled. "But not for much longer . . ."

"The Female Furies are Darkseid's elite warriors," Superman told Atheena. "Their leader is Granny Goodness, but there is nothing good about her! Do not underestimate them!"

The Female Furies swarmed over Superman. They tried to overcome him with their strength and numbers, but the Man of Steel stood his ground.

WHAM!

Superman flung his arms wide and the warriors were thrown aside.

"Lashina! Mad Harriet! Double up!" Granny Goodness instructed.

CRACK!

Lashina snapped her energy whip at Superman. He caught the end of it in his fist. At the same time, Mad Harriet howled and slashed at the Man of Steel with her razor-sharp claws.

CRUNCH!

Mad Harriet's claws broke against his invulnerable body. Superman twirled Lashina around and around.

At last, Superman let go. Mad Harriet went sailing away into the distance.

"He's distracted! Fire, Artemiz!" Granny ordered.

ZIP!

A Female Fury with a glowing bow shot an arrow at the Man of Steel. It was not an ordinary arrow. It had a kryptonite tip!

WOOOOOSH!

Superman dodged just in time. Then he blew a gust of his super-breath and sent Artemiz soaring in the same direction as Lashina.

"Bernadeth! Stompa! Gilotina! Team up!" Granny Goodness said. Then she saw Superman doing something that made her hesitate.

SWOOOOOSH – WOOOOOSH – SWOOOOOSH!

The Man of Steel was flying in a circle around the Fire Pit. He created a vortex of flame and sent it straight toward Granny Goodness. In a panic, she turned and zoomed far away, barely escaping the tendrils of fire.

Darkseid watched Granny's humiliating retreat on the holographic monitors. "Coward!" the Dark Lord growled.

Suddenly a muscular man with pointed ears and a permanent frown ran into the room. "Father! Apokolips is under attack!" Kalibak shouted in alarm.

Darkseid turned to face his agitated son

and swept his arm in the direction of the holographic battle. "I know that already, you fool!" Darkseid snarled.

Kalibak looked at the images. He watched Superman battle the Female Furies. He saw the battle robots fighting the Parademons. Hundreds of rebels fought for freedom on the streets of Apokolips.

Kalibak looked at Darkseid sitting on his throne. "So, what are you going to do about it?" he asked. Kalibak didn't understand why Darkseid sat on his throne and watched the holographic images of Superman and the rebels fighting the Parademons and Female Furies. "Why do you let your warriors battle when you could easily crush the rebels?" he asked.

"Insolent fool!" Darkseid roared. "You dare question me?"

Kalibak cowered. "N-no, Father! I-I only wonder . . ." the son of Darkseid stammered.

"My warriors fight because I command them! They exist to obey me!" the Dark Lord declared. "They do not question! They do not wonder."

Darkseid glared at Kalibak with red, glowing eyes. Kalibak feared that his father was about to unleash his devastating Omega Beams, so Kalibak bowed and retreated from the room, his shoulders bowed more than usual.

"I am Darkseid's son and he does not call upon me to fight!" Kalibak grumbled. "I am a worthy warrior! I'll just have to show him my superior skills. I will win the battle for Darkseid. Then my father will respect me!"

Kalibak returned to his room and prepared himself for battle.

CHAPTER 5

ALL OR NOTHING

Kalibak stepped onto a pair of aero-discs. He flew out of Darkseid's fortress and headed toward the battle.

"Fool," Darkseid muttered as he sensed Kalibak leave.

The Dark Lord continued to watch the conflict on the holographs. One of the images showed Kalibak flying as fast as a missile toward Superman. Kalibak screamed his battle cry as he rushed at the Man of Steel.

"YAAAAAA!"

The sound alerted Superman to the oncoming threat. He turned to see Kalibak coming at full speed. The Man of Steel moved aside at the last moment and let Kalibak pass by.

WHAM!

Kalibak crashed into the side of a building.

Piles of rubble fell on Kalibak and covered him. A few seconds later, the mound shifted as if an earthquake rumbled below it. Suddenly all the rocks and debris exploded outward.

CRACK!

Kalibak used his Beta-Club to blast away the rubble and free himself. He was embarrassed. He missed his very first attack on the enemy.

This made him angry. He flew into the sky once more and took aim at Atheena's robot.

Kalibak and the Female Furies surrounded Superman and Atheena's damaged robot. They aimed their powerful weapons at him. They were sure he was finished fighting.

"Do the robot's boosters work?" Superman whispered to Atheena through his radio.

"Yes," she said.

"Get ready to use them," the Man of Steel told her.

To Kalibak and the Furies, Superman said, "What are you waiting for? Fire!"

Trained only to obey commands, Kalibak and the Female Furies fired their weapons by instinct.

ZA-POWWWW!

Energy beams streaked like lightning at the Man of Steel. Before the beams struck, Superman tossed Atheena's battle robot high into the air. The boot boosters flared to life. She was clear of the onslaught.

ZAP!
WHACK!
BOOM!
DOOM!

The Man of Steel hovered in midair next to the unconscious bodies of Kalibak and the Furies. He had tricked them into shooting at each other and knocking themselves out!

At super-speed, Superman grabbed some metal girders from the ruined buildings and wrapped up his foes with the metal.

FWOOSH!

The Man of Steel threw their makeshift cage far over the horizon. "They won't be back anytime soon," Superman said.

Suddenly Superman heard a tremendous BOOM! An energy portal opened nearby.

"Dr. Zox did it!" Atheena said. "He used the Grandmother Box to open a Boom Tube!"

"Everyone! Get into the Boom Tube!" Superman shouted to the rebels.

"Battle robots, form a perimeter!" Athena commanded. "Protect the fighters on the ground!"

Parademons streaked toward the fleeing rebels. Superman placed himself between Darkseid's warriors and Atheena's freedom fighters.

SIZZZZZLE!

His heat vision melted the Parademons' weapons.

KA-POWWW!

A punch knocked down the warriors and scattered them. More and more rebels ran into the Boom Tube.

The rebellion was succeeding!

UNTIL...

Superman followed Darkseid through the sky over Apokolips. It was a never-ending city. The whole planet was covered with buildings and massive Fire Pits.

Darkseid had smashed into the tops of several tall structures before he recovered his balance.

Superman delivered a second super-powered blow.

CRACK!

He had to keep Darkseid distracted so the rebels could escape!

SMAAAAASHHH!

The Man of Steel plowed into Darkseid like a freight train.

CRAHHACKKK!

The ruler of Apokolips hit the street so hard that a giant crack opened in the ground.

RUUUUUMMMMBLE!

Tremors shook the buildings.

The Man of Steel did not give his opponent a chance to recover or retaliate. He pulled Darkseid up out of the chasm and threw him into a Fire Pit! Darkseid was not harmed by the flames.

"Superman!" Atheena said in his earpiece. "Everyone is through the Boom Tube. You and I are the only ones left. Get back here!"

Darkseid was surprised to see the Man of Steel turn and fly away.

"Coward," the evil ruler snarled as he fired twin Omega Beams at the retreating Kryptonian.

ZAP-ZAP!

WOOOOOSH!

Superman flew at super-speed back toward the Boom Tube. The Omega Beams were right behind him! He knew if he got hit, he would lose his chance to escape Apokolips.

The Man of Steel saw Atheena standing in the Boom Tube. He was almost there, but so were the Omega Beams!

ZOOOOOM!

Superman soared even faster.

SWOOOOOSH!

He grabbed Atheena as he passed.

BOOOOOM!

The energy portal closed with a tremendous roar.

Superman and Atheena were tossed out the other side of the Boom Tube onto a sandy beach. The portal closed behind them.

Superman thought he heard ringing in his ears. Then he realized it was the sound of the rebels cheering.

"Thank you, Superman," Atheena said. "We'll be safe here."

"Nice planet," Superman said as he looked around at the tropical paradise.

"Dr. Zox will open the Boom Tube and send you home when you're ready," Atheena said.

Superman looked out at the seashore. "I think I'll stay here for a while," he said. "Compared to Apokolips, this is a day at the beach."

BIOGRAPHIES

Laurie S. Sutton has read comics ever since she was a kid. She grew up to become an editor for Marvel, DC Comics, Starblaze, and Tekno Comix. She has written Adam Strange for DC Comics, Star Trek: Voyager for Marvel, plus Star Trek: Deep Space Nine and Witch Hunter for Malibu Comics. There are long boxes of comics in her closet where there should be clothing and shoes. Laurie has lived all over the world, and currently resides in Florida.

Luciano Vecchio was born in 1982 and currently lives in Buenos Aires, Argentina. With experience in illustration, animation, and comics, his works have been published in the US, Spain, the UK, France, and Argentina. His credits include Ben 10 (DC Comics), Cruel Thing (Norma), Unseen Tribe (Zuda Comics), and Sentinels (Drumfish Productions).

SKETCHES

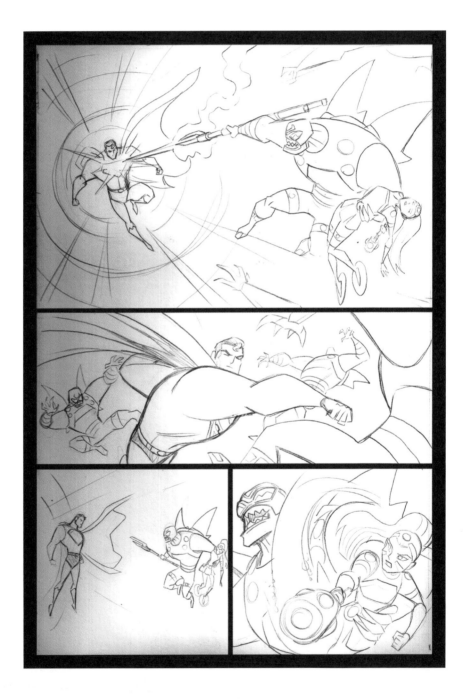

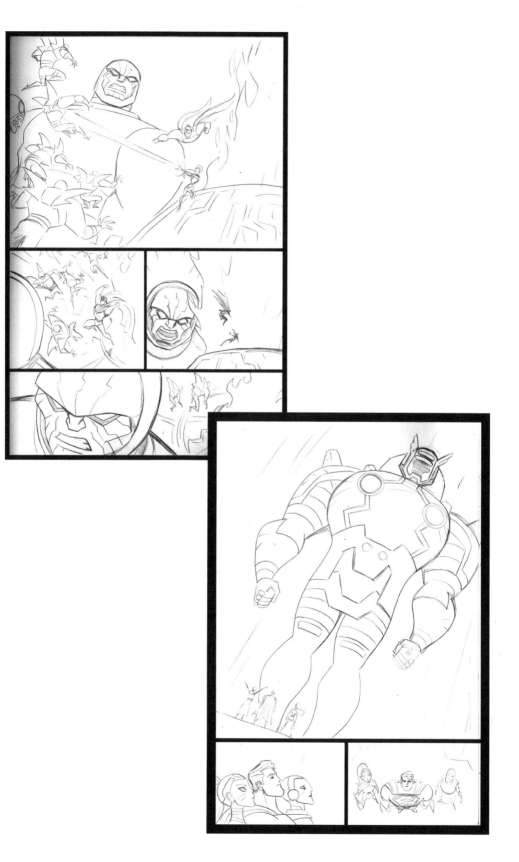

COMICS TERMS

caption (KAP-shuhn)—words that appear in a box. Captions are often used to set the scene.

gutter (GUHT-er)—the space between panels or pages

motion lines (MOH-shuhn LINES)—illustrator-created marks that help show motion in art

panel (PAN-uhl)—a single drawing that has borders around it. Each panel is a separate scene on a spread.

SFX (ESS-EFF-EKS)—short for sound effects. Sound effects are words used to show sounds that occur in the art of a comic.

splash (SPLASH)—a large illustration that often covers a full page (or more)

spread (SPRED)—two side-by-side pages in a comic book

word balloon (WURD BUH-loon)—a speech indicator that includes a character's dialogue or thoughts. A word balloon's tail leads to the speaking character's mouth.

GLOSSARY

crucial (KROO-shuhl)—extremely important or vital

disintegrated (diss-IN-tuh-gray-tid)—to break apart into many small parts or tiny pieces

hesitate (HEZ-uh-tate)—to stop briefly before you do something

invulnerable (in-VUHL-ner-uh-buhl)—unable to be harmed or damaged

maintenance (MAYN-tuh-nuhnss)—the act of keeping property or equipment in good condition by making repairs

modifications (mod-if-uh-KAY-shuhn)—changes made to the parts of something

onslaught (ON-slot)—a violent attack

surged (SERJD)—to move very quickly and suddenly in a particular direction

tyranny (TEER-uh-nee)—cruel and unfair treatment by people with power over others

tyrant (TIE-ruhnt)—a ruler who has complete power over a country and who is cruel and unfair

VISUAL QUESTIONS

1. This panel shows Darkseid's eyes glowing set against a black silhouette of his face. How do you feel when you see this panel? Why did the illustrator draw it this way?

2. Darkseid's Omega Beams can turn at right angles to follow their target. Whose powers would you rather have, Superman's or Darkseid's?

3. Why are there multiple shots of Superman in this panel? Explain your answer using text from the story.

4. Atheena and Superman make a good team. Find a few examples of how they helped each other in this book. Write down the ones you find.